pic 2617107

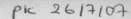

Airy Fairy

Magic Mistakes!

Look out for more stories...

Magic Mischief!

Magic Muddle!

Magic Mess!

Magic Mix-up!

Magic Mistakes!

Margaret Ryan

illustrated by Teresa Murfin

■ SCHOLASTIC

To Jessie, with love

Scholastic Children's Books,
Euston House, 24 Eversholt Street,
London NW1 1DB, UK
a division of Scholastic Ltd
London ~ New York ~ Toronto ~ Sydney ~ Auckland
Mexico City ~ New Delhi ~ Hong Kong

First published by Scholastic Ltd, 2005

Text copyright © Margaret Ryan, 2005
Illustrations copyright © Teresa Murfin, 2005

10 digit ISBN 0 439 96338 9
13 digit ISBN 978 0439 96338 1

Printed and bound by Nørhaven Paperback A/S, Denmark

6 8 10 9 7 5

Chapter One

It was the last night of the summer holidays at Fairy Gropplethorpe's Academy for Good Fairies, and Airy Fairy had made herself a promise.

"Tomorrow is the beginning of the new term," she said to pocket Ted, "and I'm going to try really hard not to be at the bottom of the class. For a start, I'm going to be first at assembly. Miss Stickler should be pleased about that."

Airy Fairy set her little alarm clock for early and placed it on her chest of drawers. On the chair beside her bed she laid out her clean school frock, her clean school socks and her clean school shoes.

Then she climbed into her little fairy bed, said goodnight to Ted, and fell asleep. After a while, she started to dream. It was a really nice dream. She dreamed that she got all her sums right. She dreamed that she got all her spelling right. She even dreamed that she was the best at flying in the whole fairy class.

She could glide through doorways without bumping her nose or bending her wings. She could fly backwards without banging into walls or crashing into trees. She could even hover gracefully in the air like a fairy should without yelling, "Help, I'm falling! Somebody catch me!" And her wings stayed shimmery and shiny instead of being covered in bits of sticking plaster, like they usually were. Miss Stickler was really pleased with her and Fairy Gropplethorpe was delighted. Fairy Gropplethorpe was just patting her on the shoulder when...

"Airy Fairy!" Her friends, Tingle and Buttercup, shook her shoulder. "Wake up, wake up! You're going to be late for school. Didn't you set your alarm clock?"

"Whaaat?" Airy Fairy jumped out of bed, slid on the rug and banged her head on the floor. "What time is it? I set my alarm clock for early. I know I did." 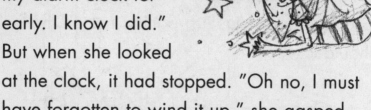 But when she looked at the clock, it had stopped. "Oh no, I must have forgotten to wind it up," she gasped.

"Don't worry about that now," said Tingle.

"Just hurry up," said Buttercup. "It's assembly in the hall today. We'll keep you a place beside us."

Airy Fairy flew along to the bathroom and splashed her face with water. Then she

hurried back to her room and threw on her
school uniform.

"At least my clothes are nice and clean,"
she said, and flew downstairs. She was just
about to go into the assembly hall when she
heard some frantic barking coming from the
school kitchen.

"That's Macduff." She frowned. "He
doesn't usually bark like that. I'd better go
and find out what's wrong. I don't have
much time, but there might be a problem."

There was. Airy Fairy found Macduff standing in the middle of the kitchen floor barking at Rainbow, Fairy Gropplethorpe's kitten. She was standing in the middle of a puddle of treacle, completely stuck.

"Oh, poor Rainbow," said Airy Fairy, and knelt by the edge of the puddle to try to rescue her. But she couldn't quite reach. She stretched forward a little. But she still couldn't reach. She stretched forward a little more. "Oh no," she gasped as her fairy frock dipped into the treacle. "Just look at the mess!" Then she clutched at her frock and toppled into the treacle herself.

"Help!" she cried. "Now I'm stuck too." But, after much huffing and puffing, she managed to grab hold of Rainbow and unstick them both.

"Well, Rainbow," she panted as she sat back on the clean floor. "I know you're a very curious little kitten, but please don't do that again. Treacle is very sticky stuff."

Airy Fairy washed the kitten as best she could, then hurried along to assembly.

"Perhaps no one will have noticed I'm late," she said hopefully. But they had.

"There you are at last, Airy Fairy," said Miss Stickler, frowning. "Late as usual. I thought even you might manage to be on time on the first day of term, but obviously not. I was just about to send Scary Fairy to search for you. SHE arrived early and helped to put out the chairs for assembly. And just look at the state of you! Your frock and your socks and shoes are filthy. Where on earth have you been?"

Scary Fairy smirked. "Probably making mud pies in the garden with that red squirrel she's so fond of," she said. Scary Fairy was Miss Stickler's niece and Airy Fairy's worst enemy. "No, I wasn't, I…"

"There's no time for excuses," snapped Miss Stickler. "Here comes Fairy Gropplethorpe. Go and take your place. I'll deal with you later."

"Yes, Miss Stickler," sighed Airy Fairy. It was always the same. No matter how hard she tried, she never seemed to do anything right, and it looked like this term would be no different.

Airy Fairy took her place beside Buttercup and Tingle as Fairy Gropplethorpe climbed up on to the platform.

"Good morning, Fairies," she said, beaming. "How nice to see you all looking so bright and clean this fine morning."

"Not quite all, I'm afraid," replied Miss Stickler, frowning, "but I shall speak to Airy Fairy later."

"Ah, Airy Fairy," said Fairy Gropplethorpe. "Will you come up here a moment, please?"

Airy Fairy gulped and went up on to the platform. She rubbed nervously at the sticky brown patches on her frock. She didn't like to make Fairy Gropplethorpe cross.

"I'm sorry I'm in a bit of a mess, Fairy Gropplethorpe..." she started to explain.

But Fairy Gropplethorpe held up her hand for silence then wiped a finger over Airy Fairy's frock. After that, she did a strange thing. She licked her finger.

"Ah, just as I thought," she said. "Treacle."

"Oh no! Airy Fairy's been stealing treacle from the school kitchen!" exclaimed Scary Fairy.

"No, I haven't, I was…"

"I know exactly what you were doing, Airy Fairy." Fairy Gropplethorpe smiled. "You were rescuing Rainbow." And she dived into her big bag and brought out a slightly damp, slightly sticky kitten, still smelling faintly of treacle.

Airy Fairy grinned. "She just made a little mistake. She knocked over the treacle tin and the treacle went all over the floor. Then she got stuck in it and so did I. I tried to clean her up."

"Just as I thought," replied Fairy Gropplethorpe, smiling. "Well done, Airy Fairy, that's just the kind of thing a good fairy should do. You've made a very good start to the autumn term."

Scary Fairy scowled while the other fairies clapped. Airy Fairy laughed and went back to her seat.

"Well done, Airy Fairy," whispered Buttercup and Tingle.

"Now," went on Fairy Gropplethorpe, putting Rainbow back into her big bag. "I have some news for you."

"Oh, I hope it's not about doing loop the loop flying lessons this term," worried Airy Fairy. "I still can't manage flying through revolving doors."

But it wasn't about that.

"I've had a letter from Fairy Noralot, the chief inspector of schools," said Fairy Gropplethorpe. "And she wants us to study an extra subject this term."

"I knew it," muttered Airy Fairy. "It's definitely looping the loop. I'll never manage it. I'll get dizzy. I'll get sick. I'll get…"

"You'll get extra homework if you don't keep quiet and pay attention to Fairy Gropplethorpe," hissed Miss Stickler behind her.

Airy Fairy kept quiet, but she didn't stop worrying.

"And the extra subject is…" Fairy Gropplethorpe paused, "…cooking."

"Yummy," cried some of the other fairies.

"There's a lot of fruit in the garden at this time of year, and Fairy Noralot wants it put to good use. She wants you to learn some new cooking spells."

"Oh no," gasped Airy Fairy. This was even worse than learning to loop the loop. She was hopeless at cooking. When she had been in charge of the porridge pot on their school camping holiday, the porridge had escaped from the pot and splashed all over her.

"And to make things even more interesting," added Fairy Gropplethorpe, "Fairy Noralot has organized a cooking competition with Fairy Topnob's school. The fairy who produces the best food will win a special dinner for everyone in her school at

Gobbler Goblin's restaurant. Gobbler Goblin himself has kindly agreed to do the judging. Isn't that exciting? You'll be cooking for a famous chef."

"Oh no," gasped Airy Fairy again. Gobbler Goblin was the eldest son of Mr and Mrs Goblin, and was known to be a bit grumpy. "I'm sure he'll be even stricter than Miss Stickler," she muttered to Buttercup and Tingle, "and I'm sure to get the new cooking spells in a muddle. I'm sure to make lots of mistakes."

"Stop worrying, Airy Fairy." Buttercup and Tingle tried to soothe her. "You'll be fine."

"Oh no, you won't," muttered Scary Fairy to herself. "I'll soon see to that. I'm the cleverest fairy around here and I'm going to win that competition myself."

Chapter Two

"We will begin our new cooking lessons right away," said Miss Stickler to the fairies when they were back in their classroom. "And we'll start by collecting the fruit from the garden."

Airy Fairy looked out of the classroom window at the apple tree that grew nearby. The red apples on it were nearly as big as she was.

"I'll hardly be able to LIFT one of those apples, never mind cook with it," she worried. "And look at the size of the pears on the pear tree. They're enormous." Airy Fairy craned her neck to see what else there was in the garden. She was just trying to count the number of plums on the plum tree when Miss Stickler called out, "Airy Fairy, will you stop gazing out of the window and pay attention."

"Yes, Miss Stickler. Sorry, Miss Stickler," said Airy Fairy, and put on what she thought was a paying-attention face. She narrowed her eyes and stared hard at Miss Stickler.

"And stop making silly faces. I never met such a girl for making silly faces."

"Yes, Miss Stickler. Sorry, Miss Stickler,"
said Airy Fairy, then wondered what to do
with her face. She propped it up on her
hands, and...

"And take your elbows off the desk and sit
up straight. I never met such a girl
for lounging and sprawling."

"Yes, Miss Stickler. Sorry,
Miss Stickler," sighed Airy
Fairy. *Sometimes it's very
difficult being a fairy*, she
thought. *I wonder if it's any
easier being a red squirrel?*
Out of the corner of her eye (she was scared
to move her head in case Miss Stickler
caught her) she could see the red squirrel,
jumping about among the branches of the
oak tree where the school was perched.
To passers-by, the school just looked like an
abandoned tree house, but inside it was
home to ten tiny orphaned fairies.

"You will need to learn some new spells before we go down into the garden," Miss Stickler continued. "We haven't done any fruit spells before."

And she began writing an apple spell in the air with her teacher's wand...

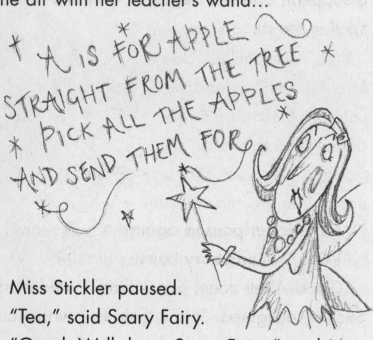

A IS FOR APPLE
STRAIGHT FROM THE TREE
PICK ALL THE APPLES
AND SEND THEM FOR

Miss Stickler paused.

"Tea," said Scary Fairy.

"Good. Well done, Scary Fairy," said Miss Stickler, beaming. "Now, Fairies, I want you all to learn that spell off by heart."

"I know it already," boasted Scary Fairy.

Miss Stickler left the spell written in the air while the fairies learned it. Airy Fairy gazed up at it and repeated it to herself till she was sure she knew it. Then, with a wave of her wand, Miss Stickler made the apple spell disappear, and she began to write the pear spell in the air...

P IS FOR PEAR
YELLOW AND PINK
SEND THEM TO ME
QUICK AS A

Miss Stickler paused again.

"Wink," cried Scary Fairy.

"Good. Well done, Scary Fairy," said Miss Stickler, delighted. "Now, Fairies, I want you to learn that spell off by heart too."

"I know it already," boasted Scary Fairy.

Miss Stickler left the spell written in the air while the fairies learned it.

Airy Fairy read the spell over and over, then she repeated it to herself till she was sure she knew it. Then, with a wave of her wand, Miss Stickler made the pear spell disappear and began to write the plum spell in the air...

P IS FOR PLUM
PURPLE AND RED
SEND THEM ALL DOWN
TO MAKE JAM FOR MY

Miss Stickler paused once more.

"Bread," cried Scary Fairy.

"Good. Well done, Scary Fairy!" cried Miss Stickler. "Now, Fairies, I want you to learn that third spell."

Airy Fairy blew out her cheeks. This was really hard work for the first day of term. She read the spell over and over, then repeated it to herself till she was sure she knew it. Just to be certain, she closed her eyes and repeated it to Buttercup and Tingle too.

"Well done, Airy Fairy," they said. "You've got it."

Airy Fairy beamed. Perhaps these new cooking lessons wouldn't be so bad after all.

"Time's up, Fairies," said Miss Stickler. "You should know all the spells off by heart by now, so bring your wands with you and follow me down into the garden."

The ten fairies flitted along the corridor behind Miss Stickler.

"I wonder what dishes we'll be able to make with the apples?" said Buttercup and Tingle.

"We could try an apple pie," said Silvie and Skelf.

"Or an apple crumble," said Twink and Plink.

"Oh, they're far too easy," scoffed Scary Fairy. "I'm going to make apple turnover with spiced apple sauce."

"Oh." The other fairies fell silent. That sounded hard.

"Perhaps it'll be easier to make something with the pears or the plums," said Honeysuckle.

"Like a pear flan," said Cherri.

"Or some plum jam," said Airy Fairy. "I like plum jam."

"Oh, that would suit you, Airy Fairy," said Scary Fairy. "You're always getting in a jam. But jam won't win the cooking competition. Jam-making's for idiots, just like you." And she poked Airy Fairy with her wand.

Airy Fairy poked her right back.

Miss Stickler turned round and caught her.

"Airy Fairy," she said. "How often have I told you not to poke poor Scary Fairy with your wand? No wonder your wand is always bent. No wonder you're at the bottom of the class. There will be extra homework for you tonight, even if it is the first day of term!"

"Yes, Miss Stickler," sighed Airy Fairy. "But I really didn't start it. I..."

But Miss Stickler wasn't listening. She led the fairies to the front door of the school and flew with them down into the garden. "We shall go to the apple tree first," she said.

"Each of you must point to a branch, say your spell and wave your wand. Then the apples from that branch will arrive safely in the kitchen for you to cook with. Now off you go."

Airy Fairy looked up at the apple tree. It was covered in rosy red apples.

She pointed her little wand at a branch and wondered, *Now what was the apple spell again?*

She closed her eyes and thought very hard. "Got it," she said.

A is for apple
Straight from the tree
Pick all the apples
And send them to me.

But that wasn't quite right...

BOOF! All the apples fell down on top of Airy Fairy and knocked her over.

"Help!" she yelled. "It's raining apples!"

All the other fairies, except Scary Fairy, giggled. They just loved Airy Fairy. She was so funny.

"Airy Fairy!" Miss Stickler scowled as Airy Fairy climbed out from under the apples. "I might have known it would be you. If there's a wrong way to do something, you'll find it."

"Sorry, Miss Stickler," replied Airy Fairy, catching her breath. "It was just a little mistake."

"Well, all the other fairies' apples have arrived safely in the kitchen, and we haven't any more time to spend here. You'll just have to carry your apples to the kitchen later. Perhaps that will make you more sensible."

"Idiot," hissed Scary Fairy in Airy Fairy's ear.

"Don't listen to her," said Buttercup and Tingle. "We'll help you carry the apples."

The fairies all trooped behind Miss Stickler as she headed to the pear tree. Airy Fairy looked up at it. It was nearly as tall as the apple tree and was covered in bright golden pears tinged with pink.

Airy Fairy pointed her little wand at a branch and wondered, *Now what was the pear spell again?* She closed her eyes and thought very hard. "Got it," she said.

P is for pear
Yellow and Pink
Send them all down
To me, I think.

But that wasn't quite right...

CRUNCH! All the pears fell down on top of Airy Fairy and knocked her over.

"Help!" she yelled. "It's pelting pears!"

All the other fairies, except Scary Fairy, giggled.

Scary Fairy frowned. "I don't know why you all like her so much," she muttered. "She's such an idiot. She never gets anything right."

"Well, Airy Fairy?" Miss Stickler stood in front of her with her hands on her hips. "What happened this time?"

"Just another little mistake, Miss Stickler," said Airy Fairy. "But it won't happen again. I'm sure I know the correct spell for the plum tree."

And she went over to the plum tree, pointed her little wand at a big cluster of plums and said...

But then she paused just long enough for Scary Fairy to hiss...

PLOP! PLOP! PLOP!
The plums plummeted down on top of Airy Fairy and knocked her over.

"Help!" she cried. "Plum attack! Plum attack!"

Miss Stickler flew over right away and found Airy Fairy sitting in among the plums. Her wings were bent, her wand was wonky, and her fairy frock was covered in purple plum juice.

"Just another little mistake, I suppose, Airy Fairy," yelled Miss Stickler.

"No, Miss Stickler. I mean, yes, Miss Stickler. I mean, I don't know how it happened, Miss Stickler," gasped Airy Fairy.

"The plums came down before I had finished saying the spell, and I was sure I was going to get it right too."

"Well, you obviously didn't. I don't think you even tried, Airy Fairy. But you are definitely trying my patience, and if your behaviour doesn't improve, you won't even get to enter the cooking competition. Is that clear?"

"Yes, Miss Stickler," answered Airy Fairy miserably. "I promise I'll try harder."

"Huh, that won't do you any good," muttered Scary Fairy. "Not while I'm around. The winner of that cooking competition is going to be ME."

Chapter Three

Buttercup and Tingle helped Airy Fairy fly her apples and pears and plums up to the school kitchen, and the cooking lessons began.

"First," said Miss Stickler, "we have to learn the spell to peel the fruit."

"Oh dear," worried Airy Fairy. "There's such a lot of spelling this term and I'm not very good at it. It's already got me into so much trouble."

But she watched carefully as Miss Stickler
wrote the fruit-peeling spell up in the air with
her teacher's wand...

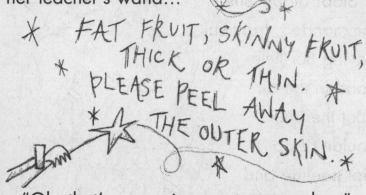

FAT FRUIT, SKINNY FRUIT,
THICK OR THIN.
PLEASE PEEL AWAY
THE OUTER SKIN.

"Oh, that's an easier one to remember."
Airy Fairy smiled, and read it over and over
till she was sure she would never forget.

Then Miss Stickler waved away the fairy
writing and the fairies all pointed their
wands at the fruit and said the spell. All of a
sudden everybody's fruit began to peel itself.
Curly strips of apple, thin strips of pear and
slippy skins of plum all dropped on to the
table.

"I did it. I did it. Mine worked," cried
Airy Fairy.

But it hadn't. Airy Fairy's fruit wouldn't stop peeling itself. It kept on and on.

"Stop! Stop!" she commanded, frantically waving her little wand in the air.

But the fruit wouldn't stop. It kept peeling and peeling till Airy Fairy was left with nothing but an apple core, a pear stump and a brown, pitted plum stone.

"Oh no," she wailed. "How can I cook with those? How did that happen? I'm sure I did the spell right."

"You did," giggled Scary Fairy to herself. "But I soon fixed that. I'm not the very best at spelling for nothing. Now you're sure to be knocked out of the cooking competition."

But she had reckoned without Buttercup and Tingle. They secretly shared their fruit with Airy Fairy, so that when Miss Stickler came to inspect their work, she had a little pile in front of her.

"That's better, Airy Fairy," said Miss Stickler as Scary Fairy scowled. "Now I'm going to hand out some fairy cookbooks with pudding recipes in them. Have a look through them and decide which ones you want to try. The basic spells are written beside them to help you. But remember, this is an inter-schools contest, so you'll have to add something to the spells to make them extra special. I'm sure Fairy Topnob's fairies will be good cooks, so you must try your very best not to let Fairy Gropplethorpe and the Academy down." And she gave Airy Fairy a stern look. "Do YOU understand, Airy Fairy?"

"Yes, Miss Stickler," gulped Airy Fairy.

"I promise I'll do my very very best."

Scary Fairy made a scary face at her. "It still won't be good enough," she whispered. "You'll be hopeless as usual."

But Airy Fairy just stuck out her tongue and picked up one of the cookbooks.

"I'll start with the apple recipes, I think," she said. "Here's one for apple crumble. It doesn't look too difficult. Perhaps I could try that." And she waved her little fairy wand and said the spell...

Slice the apples into the pot
add sugar and water, but not a lot
Cook till the apples are soft and sweet
Add crumble topping for a tasty treat

ZIP! A beautiful apple crumble appeared on the kitchen table in front of Airy Fairy.

"I did it. I did it," she cried. "I got the spell right. I made an apple crumble."

Scary Fairy paused in the middle of making her apple turnover with spiced apple sauce, and glanced over at Airy Fairy's apple crumble. It really looked nice.

"I'll soon change that," she muttered, and waved her wand.

Suddenly Airy Fairy's pudding began to slide forwards towards the edge of the table. Airy Fairy made a dash to catch it, but she was too late and it crashed to the floor.

"Oh no," she cried. "Now I've got an apple tumble! Miss Stickler will be really cross."

But the twin fairies, Twink and Plink, helped her clear up the mess before Miss Stickler could see it.

"Thank you," whispered Airy Fairy and went back to the cookbook. "Perhaps I'll have more luck with a pear recipe," she sighed.

She found one for pears baked in cream. "That recipe doesn't look too difficult," she said. "Perhaps I could try it." And she waved her little fairy wand and said the spell...

Put the pears into the dish
With butter and sugar, just a swish.
Bake till the pears are soft and hot
add a little cream. Or even a lot!

ZIP! A dish of beautiful baked pears in cream appeared on the kitchen table in front of Airy Fairy.

"I did it. I did it," she cried. "I got the spell right. I made a beautiful dish of creamy baked pears."

Scary Fairy paused in the middle of making her spicy pears in a red wine sauce and glanced over at Airy Fairy's baked pears. They looked delicious.

"I'll soon change that," she muttered and waved her wand.

Suddenly Airy Fairy's dish of pears rose up from the table. Airy Fairy made a dash to catch it, but it quickly shot away from her.

"Oh no, come back!" she cried. "Now I've got pears in the air."

But not for long. SPLAT! The beautiful pear dish fell to the floor and broke into a hundred pieces.

"Now how did that happen?" asked Cherri and Honeysuckle as they helped her clean up the mess before Miss Stickler could see it.

"I just don't know," sighed Airy Fairy as she opened up the cookbook again. "But my cooking spells aren't going at all well. Perhaps I'll have more luck with a plum recipe."

She found one for plum pie. "This one doesn't look too difficult," she said. "I'll try that." And she waved her little fairy wand and said the spell...

Slice the plums into the dish
Add sugar, no water, not even a splish.
Cover with pastry at the end
Then into the oven send.

ZIP! A wonderful plum pie appeared on
the kitchen table in front of Airy Fairy.

"I did it. I did it," she
cried. "I got the spell
right. I made a
wonderful plum pie."

Scary Fairy paused in
the middle of making her
spiced plum and soured
cream flan and glanced
over at Airy Fairy's
plum pie. It really looked nice.

"I'll soon get rid of that," muttered Scary
Fairy and waved her wand.

"Oh no, come back. Come back!" cried
Airy Fairy as her dish rose from the table. But
it wouldn't. She flew after it, but it
zigzagged across the room
and she couldn't
keep up with it.
"Help, it's going to
crash to the floor again!"
she yelled.
But it didn't.
Instead the plum pie headed
for the open window and floated outside.

"Oh no," cried Airy Fairy, rushing to the
window. "Now I've got pie in the sky!"

"What's the matter, Airy Fairy?" asked Miss
Stickler, coming up behind her.

"It's my pie." Airy Fairy pointed upwards to
the pie floating in and out among the clouds.
"I can't fly high enough yet to go and catch
it, and I don't know the spell to bring it
back."

Miss Stickler sighed.

"If there's a silly way of doing something, Airy Fairy," she said, "you'll find it." And she waved her teacher's wand and the pie came sailing back towards the kitchen.

"Oh, thank you, Miss Stickler," said Airy Fairy. "It's a really nice plum pie. I'm sure you'll like it."

But she didn't. By the time the pie settled itself back on the kitchen table a shower of rain had fallen on it and the pastry had gone soggy and cold.

"Oh no," gasped Airy Fairy. "Just look at my pie now. Sorry, Miss Stickler. Shall I make another one?"

"There's no time, Airy Fairy. We must go back to the classroom and get on with our other lessons. But I'm warning you, this cookery competition is very important to the school, and unless you pull up your socks, you will not be allowed to enter. Do you understand?"

"Yes, Miss Stickler," said Airy Fairy. She bent down and pulled up her fairy socks. "But I don't know if it'll make any difference," she sighed. "I've pulled up my socks lots of times before and it didn't help one little bit."

Chapter Four

Airy Fairy worried about the cooking competition all that day.

"How am I going to manage to cook anything for the competition when I can't even get my dish to stay on the table?" she said to Tingle and Buttercup as they sat on an oak branch at afternoon break.

"I'm sure that was Scary Fairy up to her nasty tricks," said Buttercup.

"And I know you can do it," said Tingle.

Airy Fairy smiled. "Thank you, you've made me feel much better."

But it didn't last. Before the end of afternoon school, Fairy Gropplethorpe came into the classroom wearing a frown.

"I have some more news about the cooking competition," she said.

"Has it been cancelled?" asked Airy Fairy hopefully.

"I'm afraid not, Airy Fairy," replied Fairy Gropplethorpe. "Quite the opposite. It has been brought forward to tomorrow."

"Tomorrow!" gasped Airy Fairy. "But tomorrow's ... the day after today. Tomorrow's ... tomorrow! How are we going to have time to practise our cooking spells?"

"I don't need to practise mine." Scary Fairy smirked. "They're perfect already."

"I know it's very soon," said Fairy Gropplethorpe. "But it seems that it's the only time Fairy Topnob's school can take part in the competition. Their French teacher, Fairy Liquide, is taking their entire school on a trip to France the day after."

"Then you'll just have to work extra hard, Fairies," said Miss Stickler. "I'm sure you can do it. Homework for tonight will be all about cooking spells. And you will have some extra work, Airy Fairy. I don't want you letting the school down."

Airy Fairy slumped down in her chair and blew out her cheeks. It definitely wasn't easy being a fairy.

After tea Airy Fairy took her cookbook to her bedroom to practise her spells. Rainbow and Macduff came along to watch. They watched as Airy Fairy tried the first apple spell again. She hung out of her bedroom window, pointed her wand at the apple tree and said her spell. The apples flew off the tree, in through the bedroom window, and knocked her over.

"Right," gasped Airy Fairy, and tried the cooking spell. She was really surprised when it worked, and a dish of delicious apple crumble appeared on top of her chest of drawers.

"Perhaps I'd better have a taste," she said, "to see if it's all right."

It tasted good, so Rainbow and Macduff tried it too, and scoffed the lot.

"But I don't know what I could add to it to make it extra special," said Airy Fairy. "Perhaps I should try the pear spell again."

She hung out of her bedroom window, pointed her wand at the pear tree and said her spell. The pears flew off the tree, in through the bedroom window, and knocked her over.

"I wish they wouldn't do that," gasped Airy Fairy, and tried the cooking spell. She was really surprised when it worked too, and a dish of creamy baked pears appeared on top of her chest of drawers.

Airy Fairy grinned. "I'm getting good at this, but perhaps I'd better have a taste to see if it's all right."

It tasted good, so Rainbow and Macduff tried it too, and scoffed the lot.

"Funny how the spells are working now when they didn't before," muttered Airy Fairy. "Maybe Buttercup was right about Scary Fairy. But I don't know what I could add to the pear dish to make it extra special. Perhaps I should try the plum spell again."

She hung out of her bedroom window, pointed her wand at the plum tree, and said her spell...

The plums flew off the tree, and Airy Fairy ducked. But not in time. They still knocked her over.

"There must be an easier way of doing this," she gasped, and tried the cooking spell.

She was really surprised when it worked, and a dish of delicious plum pie appeared on top of her chest of drawers.

"Perhaps I'd better have a taste," said Airy Fairy, "to see if it'sall right."

It tasted good, so Rainbowand Macduff tried it too,and scoffed the lot.

"Well," Airy Fairy smiled at them, "those puddings tasted lovely. But I still don't know what I could do to make them extra special. Have you two got any ideas?"

But Rainbow and Macduff, stuffed full of food, had snuggled down on Airy Fairy's bed and were fast asleep.

"Oh well," she sighed. "I'll just have to hope I don't let Fairy Gropplethorpe and the Academy down. Perhaps if I keep my socks well pulled up, and my fingers, toes and eyes crossed, things will work out."

Perhaps.

Chapter Five

The cooking competition was to take place in the kitchen of Gobbler Goblin's restaurant.

"We'll fly there in single file, Fairies," declared Miss Stickler. "Fairy Gropplethorpe will be along later. Now, Airy Fairy, you stay right behind me and keep out of trouble."

"Yes, Miss Stickler," said Airy Fairy, and clutched pocket Ted anxiously. She did her very best to avoid the trees and only bumped into one on the way there.

Gobbler Goblin was waiting for them at the door of his restaurant. To human beings, the restaurant just looked like an old upturned wheelbarrow, but inside it was the best eating place around.

Fairy Topnob's Superior Fairies were already there. They were dressed in yellow gingham aprons and hats, and looked terribly superior.

"Oh." Miss Stickler frowned. "We didn't bring any aprons and hats."

"Here, put these on. And hurry up. We haven't got all day," said Gobbler Goblin.

"Oh dear," whispered Airy Fairy to Buttercup and Tingle. "He sounds even crosser than Miss Stickler." But she put on her white apron and chef's hat. The hat immediately grew and grew till it fell down over her eyes, over her nose, then covered her completely.

"Help! Get me out of here! Where did everyone go? Who put the lights out?"

"Oh look," sniggered Fairy Topnob's fairies. "It's that silly fairy from Gropplethorpe's."

Gobbler Goblin pulled off Airy Fairy's hat.

"Any more funny spelling nonsense and you're out of the competition," he growled.

Airy Fairy looked at him with big eyes and muttered, "Y-y-y-yes, Mr G-g-g-goblin. S-s-sorry, Mr G-g-goblin."

Scary Fairy smiled slyly. The hat trick had been a good one. That had got Airy Fairy in trouble right away.

The cooking competition began immediately.

Fairy Topnob's fairies' wands moved like lightning as they produced dish after dish. They made Apple Surprise covered in pink custard. They made Pear Perfection in a boat of puff pastry. They made plum fritters floating in apple sauce. Each dish was fancier than the last. Though they weren't as fancy as Scary Fairy's.

She produced an apple mountain with little pears perched on the sides and tiny plums hanging from the stalks of the pears. Rivers of syrup ran down the mountain into a lake of blueberries.

"That looks splendid, Scary Fairy." Miss Stickler beamed. "Well done." Then she turned to Airy Fairy. "I wish I could say the same to you, Airy Fairy, but you do not appear to have even started yet."

Airy Fairy looked around. Everyone else seemed to be producing the most amazing dishes. Sylvie was doing sticky toffee apples.

Skelf was working on a multi-coloured
pear flan, while Twink and
Plink were furiously
making identical plum
puddings. Everyone
seemed to be
doing something
except her.

"I just can't think of
anything special, Miss
Stickler," she sighed.

"Just do what you
can. We can always put
your dish at the back of the judging table
and hope Gobbler Goblin won't notice it."

Airy Fairy scuffed her fairy shoes and
wondered what to do. "I'll have to do
something quickly," she muttered to herself.
"Everyone else has almost finished." Finally
she decided, and waved her little wand and
said the spell...

Slice the apples into the pot
add sugar and water, but not a lot
Cook till the apples are soft and sweet
Add crumble topping for a tasty treat

ZIP! A dish of sweet-smelling apple crumble appeared on the table before her. Scary Fairy appeared at her side.

"Huh," she sneered, "is that the best you can do? Don't put it on the judging table anywhere near mine. Aunt Stickler has given mine pride of place right at the front."

Airy Fairy ignored her and put her apple crumble on the judging table near the back. It looked very insignificant beside all the other entries.

Miss Stickler looked at it. "Well, it'll have to do, I suppose, Airy Fairy. But I don't know what Gobbler Goblin or Fairy Gropplethorpe will have to say when she arrives."

Fairy Gropplethorpe arrived at the restaurant just as the judging was about to begin.

Airy Fairy hid behind Buttercup and Tingle, who had made little dishes of apple and jelly trifle.

"Your dishes do look nice," said Airy Fairy, "but I'm sure to get into trouble for mine."

"Try to stop worrying. It'll be fine," said Tingle.

Airy Fairy watched anxiously as Gobbler Goblin went along the judging table, looking and tasting.

"Perhaps he won't notice mine," whispered Airy Fairy.

But he did. He looked, he tasted and he frowned. Then he tasted again.

Finally Gobbler Goblin turned around to speak.

"Well, Fairies," he announced, "I have tasted all the dishes and made my decision. Some of them were very good and some were very bad."

"Oh dear," murmured Airy Fairy, and put her hands over her eyes. "I know he's going to complain about my apple crumble. I know he's going to say I didn't try."

Gobbler Goblin lifted up two dishes. "Here we have," he said, "the very best dish and the very worst."

Airy Fairy peered through her fingers. There was Scary Fairy's apple mountain and her apple crumble.

"I knew it. I knew it," she moaned. "Mine's the worst." And she put her hands over her ears and shut her eyes.

But her dish wasn't the worst.

Gobbler Goblin held up Scary Fairy's apple mountain. "This is the worst," he said. "It is far too fancy and sickly sweet. Whereas," he went on, holding up Airy Fairy's apple crumble, "this simple little dish makes the best use of good ingredients and tastes superb. This dish is the winner. Whose is it?"

Nobody answered.

"You've won. You've won, Airy Fairy,"
cried Tingle and Buttercup, pulling her hands
away from her ears, and pushing her to the
front.

"Oh look, it's that silly fairy again from
Gropplethorpe's. Who'd have thought it?"
sniffed Fairy Topnob's fairies. "We thought
our dishes were far superior."

As for Scary Fairy, she was speechless as she watched Gobbler Goblin dump her pudding in the bin. She stamped her foot and made such a scary face, it turned all the cream in the kitchen sour. But no one took any notice of her.

"Well done, Airy Fairy,"
said Gobbler Goblin.
"You've won dinner
for your school
at my restaurant.
But tell me, how
do you make an
apple crumble?"

"Hit it with a hammer," replied a dazed
Airy Fairy.

The other fairies and Fairy Gropplethorpe
fell about laughing.

"Oh sorry, I see what you mean," gasped Airy Fairy. "Well, first I made a few magic mistakes and all the fruit fell on top of me, then I made a few more magic mistakes and all the fruit knocked me over. Then I..."

"This sounds like a very long story," said Gobbler Goblin.

"It is." Airy Fairy grinned.

"But," said Fairy Gropplethorpe, coming over to congratulate her, "it has a really happy ending."

Meet Airy Fairy.

Her wand is all wonky, her wings
are covered in sticking plaster
and her spells are always a muddle!
But she's the cutest fairy around!

Look out for the other books
in this series...

Margaret Ryan

Airy Fairy

Magic Muddle!

How can one little
fairy get into such
BIG trouble?

■ SCHOLASTIC

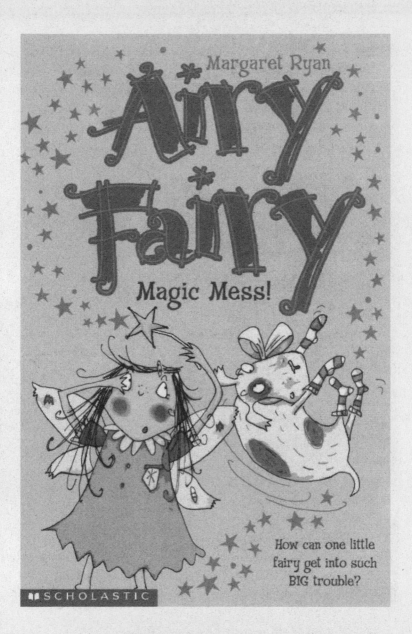

Margaret Ryan

Airy Fairy

Magic Mess!

How can one little
fairy get into such
BIG trouble?

SCHOLASTIC

Margaret Ryan

Airy Fairy

Magic Mischief!

How can one little
fairy get into such
BIG trouble?

SCHOLASTIC